by the same author
THE CHILDREN OF GREEN KNOWE
TREASURE OF GREEN KNOWE
THE RIVER AT GREEN KNOWE
A STRANGER AT GREEN KNOWE
AN ENEMY AT GREEN KNOWE

The Castle of Yew

L. M. Boston, 1892–

Illustrated by Margery Gill

HARCOURT, BRACE & WORLD, INC., NEW YORK

First American edition, 1965
Library of Congress Catalog Card Number: 65-17988

Printed in the United States of America

Contents

The Castle of Yew

ONE

Joseph Sees the Magic Garden

Joseph and a boy whom he had often seen but did not know by name stood together beside the high wire fence peering in at the garden beyond it. Their fingers clung to the wire mesh as they put their eyes close against it in order to see through the tangle of roses and honeysuckle that grew over it. There was a path on the other side, narrow and overgrown and overhung, and beyond that, glimpsed between leaves and stalks, the shine of water.

"What are you looking at?" asked Joseph.

"I'm looking for that bird that's singing. Hear it?"

Joseph listened. The bird song was cascading in soft notes of excitement and delight, with now and then a loud call, as if its joy was too great for burbling and had to be let off like a safety whistle.

"It's a magic bird," said the boy.

Joseph felt a slight shiver as he listened and thought he might be right.

3

"How do you know? Or are you just guessing?"

"I know the real birds," said the boy. "Blackbirds, thrushes, robins, wrens, and all that lot. Besides, this is a magic garden. Everybody knows that. An old lady lives in there all alone, and she can make things happen. She never goes outside the garden. But I've seen her sometimes going along that path."

"Is she frightening?"

"I wasn't frightened. But I expect you would be."

"I would like to go inside all the same."

"A boy I know went in after dark, and he said something chased him."

"Well, after dark! He ought to have known. But it looks lovely now."

"Well, if you're not afraid, go right in," said the boy. "If you meet her, you can say you are looking for a lost kitten."

"I'll say I'm collecting for hungry children. But how do I get in?"

"You go all the way round outside the garden, till you come to the riverbank. It's a long way. And then through a little iron gate there."

Joseph still peered and listened. The little path was mysterious, the rustling and movement in the bushes active and secret.

"Are you coming with me?" he asked.

"Me? No."

"Well, *I'm* going."

Inside the
Magic Garden

Joseph put his hand on the little iron gate and wondered whether he dared go any further. From this side, the garden was wide and open, the whole space laid out for long views, so that once he ventured on the path to the house where he could be seen from all the windows, there could be no hiding. It would have to be a bold approach. The path was flanked by bushes cut into strange shapes of animals and birds. There was a spread of flowers.

While he was hesitating, the postman came along on his bicycle. He stopped beside Joseph, straddling his long legs to balance the machine with its awkward piled-up carrier.

"If you are going in," he said, "be a pal and take these letters with you. It will save me a lot. The house is right off my round and no short cut to it."

Joseph never liked to say "No," so he took the letters and set off slowly up the long path. The garden was very sweet smelling,

full of happy bees. Countless birds crossed from tree to tree and sang wherever they perched, each singing his own special song so that the air vibrated with every kind of trill and whistle. Joseph began to skip and whistle, too, but checked himself in case it did not seem polite. He approached solemnly.

All the windows of the house were open. The curtains waved, and the birds flew in and out. He saw nobody moving in the rooms, nor did he hear any sound of life, hoovering or washing up or wireless.

Inasmuch as Joseph was almost trespassing or at least thinking of trespassing, you might think he would have been glad to find he had the place to himself. In fact, he didn't like the idea of being absolutely the only person there. It made much too much emptiness.

The bell was a ship's bell hanging outside the door. It would not ring discreetly somewhere away in the house but would peal and clang loudly in the open air, so that everyone in the village would know. To reach the rope, he would have to stand on the doorstep on tiptoe, and just as he put up his hand, the door opened. He found himself face to face—exactly, for they were the same height—with a little old lady. They were eye to eye, and the old lady's eyes saw uncomfortably far into Joseph's troubled stare.

She did not look like a witch. She was bent and crumpled and had hair like white straw, and her legs were as thin as a robin's.

She did not look tricky or spiteful or dangerous, but there was something about her that made Joseph anxious to be very polite.

"The postman asked me to bring your letters."

"Thank you. That was kind of you." Her voice was the only thing about her that was not old. No one could decide to take no notice of what she said. She would do very well, thought Joseph, for a fairy godmother, the one that comes after the bad ugly one and straightens things out again. He wondered what her birthday gift would be.

The old lady did not seem in a hurry to close the door. She just stood looking out at the garden and nodding her head at something that pleased her.

"I think you have a very nice garden," said Joseph. "Sometimes I look at it through the fence, but I have never been inside before."

"Have you a garden of your own?"

"Yes. It's pretty. It has sweet Williams and a sundial. But you can cross it in five hops. I mean, I can."

"I don't hop much," said the old lady.

Joseph laughed and then frowned instead of blushing. "Our garden is not very interesting. You get used to it too soon."

"Ah, yes. Five hops don't take you far. Now this garden is like a long book. You never know what you will find on the other side of the page. Would you like to explore it?"

"Yes, please. May I?"

"You may."

"Can I go wherever I like?"

"You can go anywhere you want if you really want to."

This had a slightly solemn sound, and Joseph hesitated.

"Is there anything dangerous?" he asked.

"Go on with you," said the old lady, "and find out." She closed the door.

THREE

The Yew Castle

The first thing to explore was of course the flashing water that Joseph had glimpsed through the fence. It took him quite a time to find it. Wherever he went, the garden opened out beyond him, paths led in every direction, and it took courage to venture into such strangeness quite alone while it closed round him. Empty gardens often seem to threaten an intruder, more so even than the wildest country, because they are made to be private. And who can tell whether, for instance, a tunnel cut through a dense evergreen hedge will let you through or close in and catch you in the middle? After all, bushes are alive. They stand there and wait.

Joseph remembered he had been invited and pressed on, though slowly. The twittering and whistling and fluting of the birds was so loud that it made him feel dizzy, and it drowned all other sound. He had an idea that there were many other voices he could not hear. At last he came to the water, a slow stream lying between steep banks, so that it was invisible till the top of the bank was reached. It passed between leaning trees,

close bamboo, and rushes, reflecting them all in its dark water with only an occasional mirror of bright sky between branches. It was very different from what he had imagined. It was beautiful, haunted, beckoning, and sinister. Steps led down to the water's edge, to a little platform where Joseph could stand looking in. He remembered the Grimms' fairy tale in which a quite unbearable huge face comes up out of the water and says, "Wash me!" Perhaps the platform was exactly for that. Even the picture in the book was too frightening to look at. He ran back up the steps toward the safety of the lawns but caught his foot in the ivy and fell headlong. A scolding squirrel pelted him with nut-shells, and two others joined it, shaking their long tails in so many different movements that you would have thought they had a deaf and dumb language.

Joseph picked himself up and went on. Presently he found himself facing the back of the house. Here again all the windows and doors were wide open without any sign of life. What an emptiness! Anything might happen. Anything might walk in. Anything might come out. Joseph began to move about under cover of the trees and bushes as if he were afraid—but of what?

He came to a little sunlit place where there were yew bushes cut into the shapes of chessmen set out as in a game. There were the king and queen, the bishops, the knights, and the castles.

They were all taller than himself. The empty squares on the imagined chessboard were alternately paving stones or beds of pansies.

The castles had battlements round the top. With constant clipping the walls were solid. Windows had been cut in them, and there was a door in the bastion. How safe and cozy they looked compared with that big house standing all open, with nothing moving in it but the wind and the curtains! Joseph wished with all his heart he could live in a green castle. He crouched down to the ground and laid his head on the stone to look in at the door, which was about six inches high. Through it he saw that the bush inside was hollow. He could see into a sort of round hall neatly cobbled with very small pebbles. He felt a passionate longing to go in, one of those sudden, impossible longings that bring tears to the eyes. He could have stamped and cried, but in his head he heard the old lady's voice saying, *You can go anywhere you want if you really want to.*

"All right," he said angrily, "I'm going in." He walked his two fingers in at the door and felt himself pulling in after them and gathering up into them and taking over instead of them and found the fingers turn into his whole self, and he was going in under the green arch. It was like the tunnel he had seen in the garden, but now he was not afraid; he was just madly curious.

FOUR

Company in the Castle

The cobbled hall was large, dusty, and dim, smelling very strongly of yew, which was pleasant, suggesting both log fires and stables. Joseph looked round, getting used to the green half-light. At one side of the door, dead grass cuttings had been swept like straw into a loose box. That must be where they keep the horses, he thought.

In the center of the hall, the main stem of the yew went up, and from it the branches grew out straight like rafters, bare till they reached the walls where all the leaves were crowded on the clipped twigs. From a window higher up, a shaft of light fell down in which the dust motes danced.

Joseph stepped back into the center to look at the upper part, and then he found that someone had built a light corkscrew staircase up the middle. It had been easy, because each branch grew out from the trunk a little higher up than the last in a natural spiral.

He went up. Wherever there was a window, there was a room on the level place where a branch spread its fingers. Its

16

floor was planked with dead bamboo leaves in neat rows. The first room was empty. The second faced west and had gossamer curtains looped over the window and a carpet of gold and purple pansy heads strewed evenly over the floor.

"This must be for receiving very important visitors."

The third-floor room faced south. This had a more lived-in feeling. Over the window hung two fern leaves, making a pattern like a slatted blind on the floor. They could be rolled up, back to their own curled-up shape as buds, but the sun was hot and the green blind very pleasant. There was a bed, as big as a fourposter, but it was round, made of basketwork. It was, in fact, a blackbird's nest. Joseph on tiptoes was able to look over the edge and saw inside a pillow and a coverlet made of woven grass. He had no doubt that this was a visitor's room and the bed had been made specially for him by the old-lady-fairy-god-mother. He began to sing a song of ownership, making it up as he went along:

"This is my castle,
This is my room,
This is my bed.
I have a pillow
Under my head,
I have a curtain
Of slatted gloom
To draw when I sleep in my castle."

He was interrupted by a sound of dragging and puffing downstairs. He looked anxiously over the edge of the stairs.

"Phew!" said a boy's voice. "What a weight it is!"

Joseph stood up on the stairs. "This is my castle," he said. The other boy looked round. It was Robin, who lived in the village. Joseph knew him quite well and liked him. He was older than Joseph but never bullied him.

"Hello, Jo," said Robin. "Be welcome. It's my castle really.

I am Sir Valiant of Cornwall. I was just thinking I needed a page. Come here, Page, help me to move this sack."

Joseph found this arrangement natural and pleasing. He yielded his claim to the castle and came downstairs, only making sure of his position by saying, "Pages live in the castle, don't they?"

"'Course," said Robin. "It's better with two. Come on, heave this in."

With surprise Joseph saw that the sack they were dragging along was a plastic bag of nuts and raisins. He patted his jacket pocket. It was empty. This was his bag that must have fallen out while he was lying on the ground to look through the door. It is queer to see something that was previously a mere knob in your pocket enlarged to a size that will barely go through the door. The raisins were as big as school caps, the nuts like coconuts.

"Some giant has been here," said Robin. "We must be careful. Fee fi fo fum, you know."

Joseph brushed this aside. "It was ME," he said proudly.

Robin laughed. "I wish I'd thought to leave something like that handy before I....It was sensible of you. My coat is hanging on a post where I can't get it."

Joseph knew he was being praised for something he had not meant to do, but praise is sweet. After a minute he said, "I

nearly thought of it." Then he added, "How did you get in? Oh! There it is!"

In the loose box where the litter had been bedded stood a shining, swishing, pawing horse. It was bay colored, but its long mane and tail were dark green, the color of yew trees. Anyway, the light was green, so perhaps the horse's high gloss reflected its stable.

"That's my horse," said Robin. "I wanted to play knights, and when I saw the bushes cut like horses' heads, I climbed on one and sat with my legs round its neck, and I pushed at its neck and said, 'Down, down, Emerald. Stop rearing.' And of course when it put its forefeet down, it was only half the height. And we rode across the bridge toward the castle, and the grass and the plants were growing so fast I could see them doing it. They grew higher and higher as I rode along—far above my head. It was like falling, in a dream. I was thankful to ride into the castle."

"I wish I had a horse," said Joseph.

"Can you ride?"

"No."

"Then you can do as much with this one as you could with your own if you had it. Try her with a raisin." Robin had taken off the India rubber band from the neck of the bag.

"This is yours," he said magnanimously, handing it over. "Don't lose it. It will be very useful."

22

Joseph found the rubber band wouldn't stay rolled up in his pocket, so he put it round his waist. "It's my belt," he said. He gave Emerald several raisins. She was a very friendly being, though with a quick will of her own and startling, unexpected movements.

"We'll have dinner upstairs," said Robin. "Can you eat a whole nut? That stack of buttercup petals in the corner is the plates. We throw them away after using. It's the modern way. Follow me, Page."

They went up the corkscrew staircase to the second floor, where the room had a carpet of pansies.

"Take your shoes off before you go in. People never walk on Persian carpets in shoes."

"I thought this was for very important people," said Joseph.

"Knights are very important people. This is a carpet I brought back with me from Herod's palace when I was in Jerusalem on the Crusade—very rich and silky."

Joseph rubbed his bare feet gently on the deep surface of pansy petal. A beautiful drowsy perfume arose.

They sat cross-legged with their buttercup plates on the carpet beside them. The yellow reflected from the buttercup lit up their faces like sunlight. The nuts were too big; the boys could only gnaw into them like two mice. But Robin had a penknife with which he cut raisins into slices like fruit cake. It was a very good meal.

While they ate, Joseph looked through the window and saw that from the yew-tree chess set outside, one knight was missing.

FIVE

A Monster at the Door

The nap that overtook them after their meal was interrupted by a whinny and a violent commotion from Emerald's loose box, followed by a raucous toot as from a bus close upon your heels that is not going to stop.

Leaning over the stairs, the boys saw a fierce head thrusting in at the door on a long black neck. It had heavy scarlet wattles above a beak that looked singularly good for pecking. Its body could not pass the door, but the castle walls shook from its shoving as it reached across the hall and helped itself from the sack of nuts and raisins.

"Help! It's robbing the food store! Come quickly!" Robin yelled, rushing downstairs. Joseph followed, though terrified of this great thing that swung its neck and head like a grabbing machine. Together, the boys pulled the sack round till it was behind the staircase. The moorhen jabbed at it first to one side of the central column, then to the other, and then between the stairs.

"Help! It will smash the staircase! What can we do? We

have no swords, no guns, no pepper, no soda-water syphons, no matches, no nothing!" Robin leaped about and wailed.

Joseph remembered that he had matches in his trouser pocket —absolutely forbidden, but he had not been able to resist. There had also been in his coat pocket, when he was outside the castle, a sparkler, saved (with one other treasure) from his recent birthday party. What a weapon the sparkler would have made! But it must have dropped out. It was a slippery, top-heavy thing, too long for the pocket, always falling out. He looked now toward the door. There was a bar of metal just showing, near the floor, sticking out from among the twigs.

True, the moorhen's body was there, but it was the place farthest away from the sharp eye and darting beak. Joseph sidled round by the wall, took hold of the metal bar, and pulled. Gradually he dragged it out—a piece of silvery wire as thick as a walking stick and twice as long as himself, with the gray sparkler fuel stuck on the end like a spearhead.

Robin at sight would have snatched it from him, but Joseph stamped and fought.

"It's mine! It's mine. Let go. Light it! The matches are in my pocket."

The moorhen had turned the side of its face toward them. The great glaring eye hung over them, suspicious and hostile.

There was a fizzing splutter. Robin helped Joseph to hold the launching base steady as the huge, dazzling blue-white stars

shot out and filled the green gloom. The moorhen's neck contracted into a quarter of its length with a strangled squawk and disappeared backward. There was a scattering of gravel, and a quacker of terror could be heard distancing in the bushes.

The final stars that flew sizzling out of a molten tongue were for the sole glory of the castle, where for a second they lit it up as for a great victory festival.

"Well done, Page," said Robin. "I was almost overcome by the dragon. Now we have got a spear. We must take the rest of the food upstairs. The dragon has eaten at least half. It will never do to lose all our food before we know what this country will yield. We might go hungry."

They carried the nuts and raisins upstairs an armful at a time, up and down, up and down, till Joseph's legs ached.

"And now," said Robin, "I shall mount my horse and ride out on a foray. Dangerous as the country is at all times and full of enemies, it is safest in the early afternoon. That is the time when cats sleep and when dogs are being taken for a walk on the lead by their owners. Since we are in the country of giants, we must think of these things. I will take your spear. Be sure you do not stir out till I return."

Joseph went up onto the battlements to watch him ride away. He was filled with envy. Emerald tittuped along on the flagstones with a pretty prancing and bouncing; then when she reached the rockery, she wove in and out of the boulders at a

slow canter, sliding down slopes on her haunches with her fore-feet stiff before her, but when she came to the great plains of the lawns, she went off at a fine gallop. Oh, happy Sir Valiant!

SIX

An Afternoon
Alone in the Castle

For a while Joseph was content to lean on the battlements and look out over the strange view. Now and then bumblebees flew past, droning like helicopters. Once a butterfly paused beside him on the castle roof, flaunting wings of scarlet and black that were as big as sails. Like sails they flapped lazily, wafting a smell of flower pollen, then were pressed tightly together upright and showed a quite different marble design underneath. Joseph stroked them and found that they felt like feathers. Finally the butterfly flew off, lurching to left and to right wildly like a kite but seeming to know where it was going.

The afternoon seemed long all alone in the empty castle. Joseph explored it again, looking out of all the windows. This time he found another bedroom just under the roof. It had the same rolled fern curtains and a beautiful round nest made entirely of new moss, exactly the right size for him. It had a coverlet of woven cobweb and thistledown. At one side of the nest

was a leaf of lamb's-tongue, furry side up for a bedside mat.

Joseph wanted to put something of his own in the room to show it was his. Things of one's own are homemaking. He felt in all his pockets. Matches—but he wanted to keep those with him. String, a pebble, a shell, a pencil sharpener, a birthday card with a picture of a jet airliner, a crumpled piece of gold paper that had covered a whole layer of chocolates. But as he feared, his other real treasure had rolled out.

He put the pebble and the shell on his windowsill as ornaments. Then he hung the picture of the jet on a convenient twig and sat down to look round him with pleasure. Certainly it was now his room. He put the string back in his pocket and picked up the pencil sharpener. It gave him an idea, and he went and fetched a piece of broken nut out of the sack. He pressed it into the pencil sharpener and turned. Out of the top came delicate curly slices of nut, crisp like super cornflakes. The only difficulty was that of breaking the great nuts without a hammer. He carried a nut up to the battlement and threw it down onto

the flagstone below. Success! It split in half and after that was easy to break. He cut two buttercup plates full of crisp rolls ready for when Robin should come home. In the process, eating the fragments, he became very thirsty. He put on his thinking cap—an expression he was fond of. It meant sitting with one first finger on his temple and the other pointing to the sky, as in a picture he had seen somewhere of a wise man. An idea came. He carefully straightened out his sheet of gold paper, and using his thumb to shape it as a potter would, he formed a golden cup on a stem with a round base. It had been a big sheet of gold foil and made a drinking vessel the proper size and just the thing for a knight's castle. He stood it in the middle of the room, where it looked splendid enough for King Arthur.

However, it was still empty. He did not think he could climb down the steps to the stream without Robin's help. Besides, he was even more afraid now of ugly faces surfacing and saying, "Wash me." It might be an alligator's face. When would Robin come back? He forgot that he had been told to stay indoors—and anyway, it was only by Robin, pretending.

SEVEN

Joseph
in the Pansy Wood

Joseph went out at the door in the bastion and looked round. The pansies filling an empty square in this huge chessboard were like open parasols, each tipped up to the sun to shade its stalk and roots.

Joseph began looking for his lost treasure. It was a Snake's Egg firework. When he last saw it, it had been a black ball as big as a marble, but now it would be as big as a football, though nearly weightless. The soil under the pansies was very stony. He bent down and passed underneath into their heavily scented shade.

It was a weird and magic wood to walk in, its shadow streaked with bright yellow and violet where a half-open pansy had not yet found a way up into the sun. Joseph stumbled round over roots and stones, so pleased with the place that he forgot for a while what he was looking for. By and by, as his eyes got used to the queer mixture of colored darkness and stained-glass

light, he found himself face to face with an almost invisible speckled frog as big as a fat man—face to face, that is, as far up as the wide smile, for the frog's eyes, which stuck up on the top of his head, were out of sight. He seemed to be using the out-spread surface of the flowers as if it were the top of a pond, only his eyes blinking in the light while he sat in the cool with his smile from ear to ear. Joseph had a long stare at him, his deep breathing, his deep contentment, but the frog gave no sign, his wide webbed feet spread out for anyone to tread on.

Presently Joseph moved on again, remembering to look for his egg, and where he passed, the pansy parasols swayed and showed the way he went. Before long he saw his egg, wedged in a cluster of pebbles opposite the castle door and separated from it by the width of the paving stone. He set it on the smooth surface and gave it a push toward the castle.

What was it that gave the alarm? Some little sound from the frog, or a bird or mouse that he had not even consciously heard? Perhaps just a seed dropped from a beak. Joseph was suddenly aware of great danger. He cowered under his pansy cover, from where he saw the soft round ball of his Snake's Egg roll safely in at the castle door. He peered up through the chinks of the parasol flowers and saw two eyes like round windows high above him. They were yellow and had a vertical black slit that was like a gap between curtains, and they stared terribly without any expression at the spot where he was hiding. He decided that

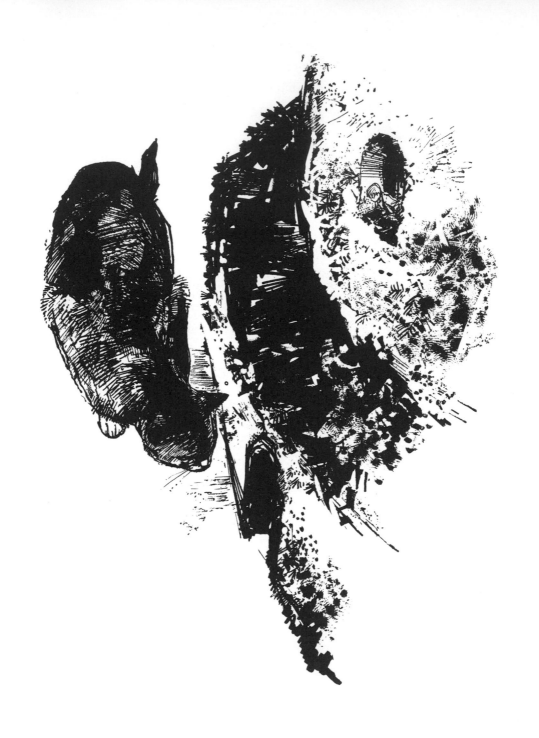

to be so high up, the cat must be on the branch of a tree—at any rate, not within striking distance, he hoped. He made a dash across the open paving stone, running faster than he ever thought he could, toward the castle, and never was mouse so glad to be back in its hole. It took him a long time to stop panting and his heart to stop pounding, but at last he went upstairs and dared to look out of the window. He saw a huge black cat crouched close to the ground and moving stealthily inch by inch to the castle door, its terrible eyes fixed on that. Fortunately, it did not seem to know about windows. It took up its position close under the walls, ready to strike round at the door if so much as a nose was poked out.

Joseph sat inside hardly breathing. He wished he was not alone. Why was Robin so long? It seemed there was no end at all to a cat's patience. It would wait, and wait, and wait. He crept up to the window to look time after time, but it never moved. Quite suddenly into his fear came another worse idea. If Robin did come back now, riding happily home the way he had gone out, he might not see the cat behind the castle till it was too late, and while he was dismounting at the door, curved hayfork claws would strike down into him and Emerald, even as she shook her beautiful skin and sighed with relief after her long ride. This was too terrible to think of, and Joseph forgot to be frightened for himself. Somehow he must get the cat away.

He searched the castle for a stick and found a good piece of dry dead twig. This he pushed out of the door once or twice just to secure the cat's attention; then he used it to push his Snake's Egg just outside the doorway, keeping himself well in the shelter of the inner wall. He was afraid the ball might roll out of reach, but it wobbled and settled just where he wanted it. On the paving outside, Joseph saw the shadow of the cat's whiskers twitch. Its nose must be very near.

It was difficult to get the end of his stick burning with matches. He used nearly all he had before it was well alight, but of course he couldn't go out to light the egg himself. He had to do it from inside with a long torch. The flame quickly blew out in the breeze, but a thin column of black smoke was rising from the egg. Then the black shiny snake, jointed like a caterpillar, was rearing itself up in coils from the egg, out of a cloud of stink-bomb fumes, and towering about the doorway. The cat's back went up. Joseph saw its high arch block out the second-floor window, but the arch collapsed in a sneeze. What the cat thought of the ghostly threatening snake cannot be known, but it sneezed seven times with a force that must almost have burst its nose. Then with deeply offended dignity it withdrew. From the battlements Joseph saw it loping away into the distance toward the village. He was glad it was not a cat that belonged here. From the battlements, too, he saw the smoke settling like a local fog over the garden beneath him. He

imagined the pansy faces frowning at the smell and wondered if it was possible for a frog face to stop smiling.

By the time the smoke had blown away, he could see Robin and Emerald returning slowly across the prairie, dragging something heavy behind him. He ran out to meet them.

"I've got a portcullis," Robin shouted.

EIGHT

A Victory Supper
in the Castle

Arrived at the castle, Robin and Joseph unharnessed Emerald and led her in. Tired as she was, she shied at the ashy skeleton of the snake at the door and could hardly be persuaded to pass it. Joseph coaxed and wheedled and boasted to her and at last brought her to her stall.

"Phew!" said Robin, too full of his own adventures to listen to Joseph's yet. "That was a good afternoon's work. I thought I had better ride all round to spy out the land. I found, far away from here, a great plantation where every row of the crops was protected against robbers with wire cages arching over the whole length. At the end of each wire tunnel is a smaller piece shaped round at the top, to block the opening. Just the right size for a portcullis, and with spikes on the bottom, too. I used Emerald's surcingle to pull it up. The hardest part was dragging it out of position. Now we can shut ourselves in safely at night."

Joseph was glad of this.

The two of them managed to drag it along on its curved edge, spikes upward. They leaned it against the inside wall of the castle by the door. It might have been made for it.

"I'm as thirsty as a dog with a mouthful of sand," said Joseph.

"Ha! Page! That's another thing. As I rode through this strange land looking to left and right, I saw a pitcher plant with pink and white jug flowers hanging from its boughs. I plucked two and brought them with me. Here they are. Tie a rope to the handle and let them down into the water from the bridge."

Joseph took with astonishment a flower almost exactly the size and shape of a china jug, except that it had a long hook instead of a looped handle. He brought out his piece of string and tied it firmly on. It proved just long enough to reach the water if he lay flat on the bridge and stretched his arms down.

The jug came up wobbly with water and splashing it out of its wide mouth. Joseph carried it home with great care.

"Come hither, Page. Give me a drink from the pitcher to quench my thirst."

"No," said Joseph solemnly. "There is SOMETHING upstairs." He staggered slowly up the stairs with grunts of concentration and successfully poured the water into the golden goblet. Then he came down again with what was left of the water for Emerald. He held the jug for her while she emptied it and licked the bottom and finally ate the jug. However, there was another, which Joseph hung up on one of those convenient twigs.

"Now you can come," he said.

"First we must make all secure for the night," said Robin. "Help me with the portcullis. You don't know what I've got for supper."

They heaved the portcullis in front of the door, jumping on the bottom rail to force the spikes into the ground so that it stood firm. Its rounded top overlapped the arch of the door. Now nothing could get in. They put the sparkler spear through from side to side for a bolt.

Deeply satisfied, they went upstairs, turning many times to look at their work.

On the carpet in the dining room stood the golden goblet and four buttercup plates, two piled with nut curls and two ready for whatever Robin should have brought.

"Guess," he said, opening his saddlebag.

"New peas?"

"Guess again."

"Clover honey?"

"No. Strawberries!" Robin produced two of these packed in moss and wrapped in violet leaves. As each was as big as a small melon, it was more than enough and looked very tempting on its gold plate.

So they sat cross-legged and passed the goblet from one to the other and banqueted after their adventures and laughed to their hearts' content in safety, while Emerald nickered sociably from below.

Last of all, Joseph told about the cat. "But it doesn't live here," he said comfortingly. "Its claws were like pitchforks."

The sun was setting, and on the battlements a blackbird was

47

singing, as loud as any saxophone. Robin stood up. "The heralds are trumpeting sundown. We must finish what we have to do. You, my brave page, have defeated the dragon and the monster and have saved the life of myself and my horse. I must make you a knight. Kneel, boy." He tapped Joseph on the shoulder with a stick. "Rise, Sir Joseph, Knight of the Fiery Stars."

After this Robin dropped his affected storybook style of talking and treated Joseph as an equal.

As they were just two boys together, they did not trouble about washing. Before it was quite dark, each climbed into his bed and continued talking from there. Joseph's was soft and sweet smelling, and he was asleep before he had finished thinking how enjoyable it was. The last thing he heard was Emerald down below getting down into her straw, a bump and a grunt as her haunches went down first, and then a happy rubbing of her head and neck in the bedding.

The Robber Squirrel

The boys were woken up by the blackbird herald on the roof of the tower. It was answered from all over the garden and from far away over the fields, although it was as yet hardly light. Joseph got up to look out of the window. The deadly chill of early morning bit into everything. Quicksilver dewdrops as big as goldfish bowls hung on every leaf and blade. No wonder the grass bent under their weight! One of those on the back of one's neck would be discouraging. He got back into his mossy bed and curled up to wait for the sun.

Later, when the dew was steaming, he still lay there because it was so comfortable and so strange. The blackbird had flown away, and in its place there was a robin, perhaps the very one in whose nest he was lying. It was singing a song under its breath that could have had words. It sounded like a long story of trouble and defiance. It was broken off in the middle of a sentence as the bird flew away.

"Robin, robin! Come back," shouted Joseph.

"What's up?" said Robin the boy from the blackbird's nest below.

To anybody outside the castle, their miniature voices must have sounded like two nestlings calling.

At that moment the castle walls began to shake. Joseph saw peering in at his window and quite filling it up a face rather like a mischievous donkey. It was worse than mischievous, it was ruthless. It chewed in anticipation.

"Robin!" shrieked Joseph. The face moved to one side, and a hairy arm shot in with bulging shoulder muscles. A leathery

hand like a gorilla's grabbed at the nest with Joseph in it and pulled it nearer.

Joseph's mouth was open, but no sound came. Shaking all over, he seized his rubber band belt, which he had taken off in the night because it was tight, and pulling it to full stretch with both hands, he let go with one. The elastic leaped to sting the attacker on the nose.

There arose a jabbering and scolding such as a shrewish old woman might make. The castle walls were shaken in anger, while the face looked in, sometimes upside down and sometimes right way up, and sometimes there was nothing but a thrashing bushy tail. Joseph aimed his elastic again and again. Then above the noise he heard steps approaching and saw the body of the old lady who lived in the house moving past his top window. Her head was out of sight, but Joseph recognized her flowered apron. She stopped. Old gnarled hands came down and picked up the enemy.

"You are a naughty squirrel," she said, taking it into her arms as if it were a household pet, scratching it under its chin. "I told you yesterday to leave that robin's nest alone. You know you took all the eggs."

Through the window Joseph and Robin watched the little bent giantess go away, feeding the squirrel with biscuits out of her pocket as she went.

TEN

Robin and Joseph Have a Big Idea

"The portcullis is no good," said Robin sadly, "unless we can have bars at all the windows, too. And yesterday when I was out riding, I saw a great poster sky high on a fence. It had letters as big as me and said BEWARE OF ADDERS."

"I want to go home," said Joseph. "But I won against the squirrel, didn't I? I wonder what we could do to get back?"

"I don't know. We both did rather babyish things to get here. Perhaps if we do something more grown up?"

"How can we, this size?"

"It will be harder."

At that moment—as if the old lady arranged that as soon as you thought of something it began to happen—a young Alsatian dog jumped clumsily over the garden gate with a bone in his mouth. He had wide floppy feet and a shiny skin so much too big for him that it slipped from side to side as he walked. He was so much bigger than an elephant that there is nothing more to say. The boys would hardly have come up to his dew claws. He trotted across the lawn and chose the best bed of flowers to bury his bone in. He began to dig, scooping the plants left and right into the air behind him and tugging the rose bushes out by the roots with tremendous contortions of his shoulders and haunches. To the boys, rose bushes were like oak trees, so that this was a very impressive sight.

"She won't like that," said Robin. "Come on. This is our chance."

They walked steadfastly through the grass, but before they got to the other side, great damage had been done. The dog was growling happily to itself as it tugged at tough roots. At the sound of the growling, Joseph dropped a little behind Robin, but when Robin in his turn faltered and looked back nervously, Joseph stepped forward.

"Bad dog," he said, as loud as he could. *"Stop it!"*

The dog stopped and seemed to listen.

"Bad dog!" said Robin, as loud as *he* could. *"Go home."*

The dog turned with a jump, looking guilty but puzzled. It sniffed the air in a circle and pointed its nose at them.

"Bad dog!" said Robin shakily.

"Bad dog!" said Joseph stoutly.

The dog advanced slowly, crouching low, and it sniffed them as it might have sniffed a bumblebee. The smell was the smell of boys! The dog wrinkled its forehead in surprise and risked a thump with its tail. It put its head on the ground in front of them and yapped.

"Look at us reflected in its eyes," said Robin. "What it is seeing is boys."

"Be off," said Joseph, advancing, "or I'll wallop you!"

The dog gave way a little.

"Shoo!"

They pursued it in this way toward the gate. On the way Robin picked up a bamboo cane to wave. It seemed a natural thing to do. He began to run. The dog barked and turned tail, but near the gate it stopped and waited for them, wagging and looking sorry.

Joseph opened the gate. "Go on, you." The dog was looking very sad, so he added, "Good dog! Go home." The dog pranced, jumped up and licked his face, and went through the gate, waiting for them on the other side as though unwilling to leave them.

Robin and Joseph, leaning on the gate, looked at each other and laughed.

"When did that happen? I didn't notice it happening."

"Neither did I! This is a nice dog. Let's go with it."

As they closed the gate, they took a farewell look at the garden. The old lady was at the front door. She waved to them and they waved back. In the chessboard garden there were two green knights.

"Next time we come," said Joseph, "I shall have a horse, too."
"Of course," said Robin.

DA